To all women who had to fight like Princess Li.
To all those who could not.
To you.

A todas las mujeres que lucharon
como hizo la Princesa Li.
A todas las que no pudieron hacerlo.
A ti.

Luis Amavisca

ÉGALITè

Princess Li / La princesa Li
Egalité Series

© Text: Luis Amavisca, 2011
© Illustrations: Elena Rendeiro, 2012
© Edition: NubeOcho and Egales editorial

www.nubeocho.com – info@nubeocho.com
www.editorialegales.com - info@editorialegales.com

English translation: Robin Sinclair
Text editing: Martin Hyams

Distributed in the United States by
Consortium Book Sales & Distribution

Second edition: 2016
First edition: 2012
ISBN: 978-84-944137-4-2
Legal Deposit: M-22367-2015
Printed in Spain – Gráficas Jalón

PRINCESS LI
LA PRINCESA LI

Luis Amavisca
Elena Rendeiro

Once **upon a time,** far away in the East, there was a **princess** named **Li.**

She and her father, **King Wan Tan,** lived in a beautiful **palace.**

Había **una vez,** en un lugar de Oriente muy lejano, una **princesa** llamada **Li.**

Ella y su padre, **el rey Wan Tan,** vivían en un bellísimo **palacio.**

Li was very pretty and everyone in the kingdom admired her beauty.

So many men wanted to marry her!

But Li was only interested in her beloved **Beatrice** who was from a **distant land.** Both were very **different,** but they loved each other more than anything.

They played in the rooms of the palace and kissed in the gardens.

Li era muy hermosa y todos en el reino admiraban su belleza.

¡Tantos hombres querrían casarse con ella!

Sin embargo ella solamente tenía ojos para su amada. Se llamaba **Beatriz** y era de una **tierra lejana.** Ambas eran muy **diferentes,** pero se querían más que nada.

Jugaban en las habitaciones del palacio o se besaban en los jardines.

Li and Beatrice were very happy until one day King Wan Tan sent for the princess.

The time had come when Li had to **get married** and she had to choose a **man from the kingdom.**

"But Dad, I want to spend **my life** with **Beatrice!"**, said Li.

Wan Tan turned red with **anger.** His daughter didn't want to marry someone from the kingdom. In fact she didn't even want to marry a man!

Li y Beatriz eran muy felices hasta que llegó el día en que el rey Wan Tan mandó llamar a la princesa.

El día de **casarse** había llegado y Li debía escoger a un **hombre del reino.**

—Pero papá, ¡yo quiero pasar **toda mi vida** con Beatriz!, respondió Li.

Wan Tan estaba rojo de **ira.** ¡Su hija no sólo no quería a alguien del reino sino tampoco a un hombre!

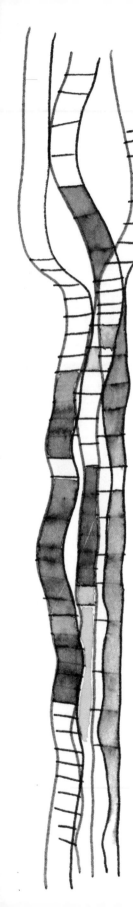

As **punishment,** Wan Tan sent Li to her room. He summoned his advisors and **Chun Bin,** the **sorcerer** of the palace.

They had to find a **solution** so that Li would **marry** a man from the kingdom.

While Li was crying inconsolably in her room, Beatrice managed to climb a **ladder** from the garden to the balcony of the Princess.

The two **hugged** each other, sad at what had happened.

Wan Tan **castigó** a Li a sus aposentos y mandó llamar a sus consejeros y a **Chun Bin,** el hechicero del palacio.

¡Tenían que encontrar una **solución** y Li se casaría con un hombre del reino!

Mientras Li lloraba desconsolada en su habitación, Beatriz desde el jardín y con la ayuda de una **escalera** consiguió subir al balcón de la princesa.

Las dos se **abrazaron** tristes ante lo sucedido.

When Wan Tan went to Li's room to talk to her, he found Beatrice there and he burst into a **rage.**

The King summoned the sorcerer Chun Bin. Li **cried and cried** in front of her father. She begged him not to **harm** Beatrice and she told him to beware of Chun Bin.

He was **evil** and just wanted the throne.

Cuando Wan Tan quiso hablar con su hija y se dirigió a su habitación, encontró a Beatriz allí y estalló en **cólera.**

El Rey mandó llamar al hechicero Chun Bin. Li **lloró y lloró** ante su padre. Le pidió que no hiciera daño a Beatriz y le advirtió sobre las intenciones de Chun Bin.

Era **malvado** y sólo quería el trono.

Wan Tan didn't listen to the cries and complaints of his daughter and ordered the **magician** to do something to **separate** the two young women.

The sorcerer muttered magic words, **strange sounds...**

and suddenly Beatrice was **transformed** into a **bird!**

Wan Tan no escuchó ni el llanto ni las quejas de su hija y ordenó al **mago** que hiciera algo para **separar** a las dos jóvenes.

El hechicero murmuró unas palabras mágicas, unos **sonidos extraños...**

¡y de repente Beatriz se **transformó** en **pájaro!**

The princess was **heartbroken.**

Her beloved was now a beautiful bird.

Nevertheless, Li and Beatrice **stayed together** the whole time.

Even now, the King could not separate them.

La princesa estaba **desconsolada.**

Su amada era ahora un hermoso pájaro.

Sin embargo, Li y Beatriz **no se separaron** en ningún momento.

Ni siquiera ahora el Rey había logrado distanciarlas.

The day came for the selection of the **new prince** at the **celebration dinner.**

Young men of the court presented themselves to Li and she had to choose under the watchful eye of King Wan Tan.

Every time one of them approached the table, the princess shook her head **in refusal.**

Llegó el día en que se celebraría la **cena** para la elección del nuevo príncipe.

Los jóvenes de la corte se presentarían ante Li y ella debía escoger ante la atenta mirada del rey Wan Tan.

Cada vez que uno de ellos se acercaba a la mesa, la princesa **negaba** con la cabeza.

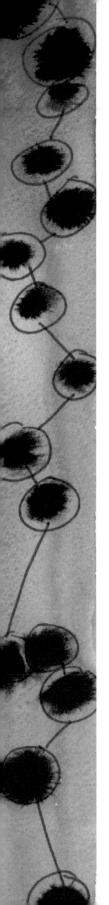

Meanwhile, the sorcerer **Chun Bin,** as Princess Li had thought, was planning to take over the **throne.** He poured a **poisonous** potion into King Wan Tan's cup.

But Beatrice the bird saw him and flew to try to **help** her king.

Although she had been transformed into a bird, she still loved Wan Tan.

Mientras tanto, el hechicero **Chun Bin,** como la princesa Li pensaba, tramaba usurpar el **trono.** Para ello vertió una pócima de **veneno** en la copa que bebería el rey Wan Tan.

Sin embargo, el pájaro Beatriz lo vio y voló para intentar **ayudar** a su rey.

Aunque Wan Tan, con la ayuda de su hechicero, la había transformado en ave, ella lo quería.

When the bird flew around Wan Tan to prevent him from drinking, the King became **angry** and tried to **hit** her.

But as he flailed about,
the cup was **knocked over** and the wine **spilled,** suddenly turning into a strange **green steaming cloud.**

Cuando el pájaro volaba alrededor de Wan Tan y no le dejaba beber, el Rey se **enfadó** e intentó golpearlo.

Pero con el **golpe,**
la copa **se derramó** y el vino se transformó de repente en un extraño **líquido verde** que echaba **humo.**

And so King Wan Tan suddenly understood everything that had happened and ordered the **arrest** of the sorcerer Chun Bin.

But before the King had him imprisoned, he forced the sorcerer to **turn** Beatrice **back** into a **girl.**

Despite what he had done to Beatrice, she had saved his life!

Entonces, el rey Wan Tan se dio cuenta de todo y mandó **apresar** al hechicero Chun Bin.

Pero antes de encarcelarlo, le obligó a **transformar** al pájaro Beatriz de nuevo en **chica.**

¡Después de lo que él le había hecho a Beatriz, ella le había salvado la vida!

And so what if princess Li loved a **girl** from **another land**?
What did it matter if it was not a **man** from the same kingdom?
Isn't **love** more important than anything?

At dinner the King decreed **the end of the selection** for a new prince.
Now the kingdom would have **two princesses.**

Y si la princesa Li amaba a una **chica** de **otra tierra,**
¿qué importaba si no era un **hombre** de su mismo reino?
¿No era el **amor** más grande que todo?

En la cena, el Rey decretó a su pueblo **el fin de la elección** del nuevo príncipe.
De ahora en adelante, el reino tendría **dos princesas.**

Beatrice and Li **got married**
and the two princesses lived **happily ever after**
in their palace with King Wan Tan.

Beatriz y Li **se casaron,**
y las dos princesas fueron **felices para siempre**
en su palacio junto al rey Wan Tan.

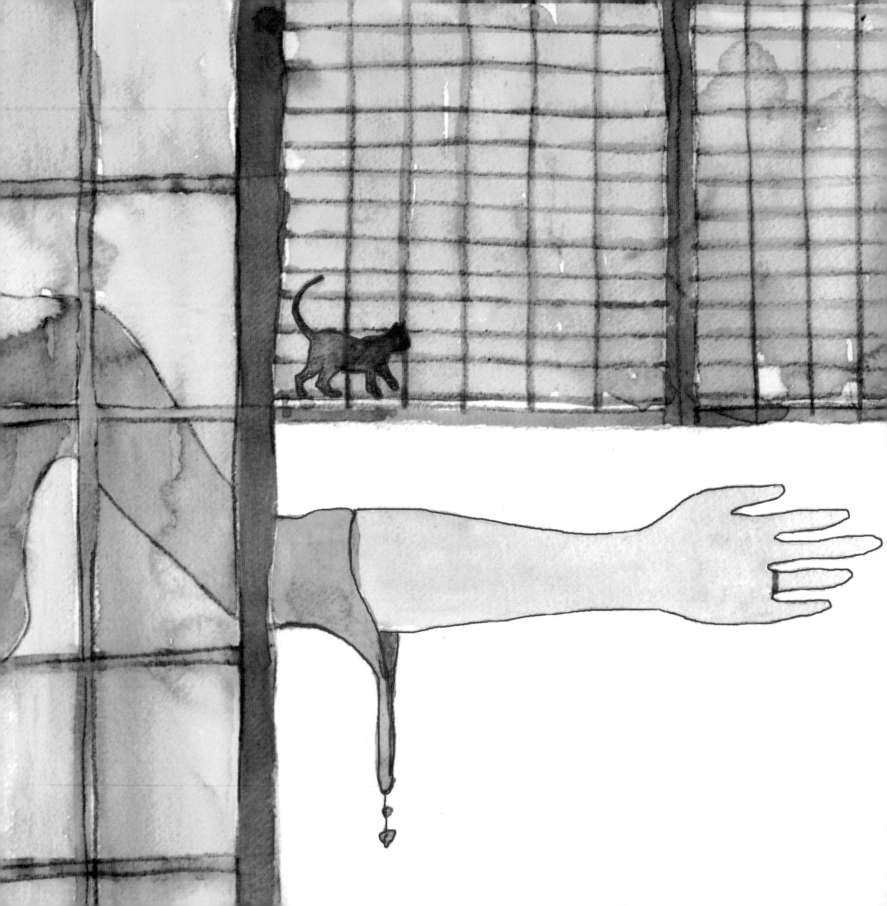